This book can be tokenized Scan the code to claim the digital token.

# Hummingbird Lily

## A fast flapping foray

*Happy reading and always be curious!*

*Deborah Ades*

## Illustrated by Deborah Ades
## Story by Deborah Ades and Simon Mills

ISBN: 9781637610237
Library of Congress Control Number: 2021944448

The summer was hotter
than boiling hot water
and Lily was bored through and through

Her friends disappeared
off to camp far from here
and Lily had nothing to do

Lily's dad had a den
not just papers and pens
but full-up with fascinating stuff

She rummaged around
then suddenly found
a suitcase all covered in dust

She undid the straps
and threw the lid back,
a dusty explosion of things

What first caught her fancy
and made her heart dancy
was a pair of far-looking rings

She wiped off the dust
with her shirt, in a rush
    and held them up close to her eyes

    Her mouth opened wide
    and so did her eyes
as she ran to see what was outside

Her eyes were fixated
Her senses, elated
    stunning red, yellow, and, green

    There in the flowers
with precision and prowess
was the fastest wing-flapping she'd seen

To the library she scuttled
and over books huddled
carefully studying each word

Excited to find
within every line
secrets of the sweet hummingbird

Lily learned from the writing
that her very first sighting
was a male hummingbird of the species

He was called "Ruby-Throated"
for his throat was so coated
and his feathers were colored so sweetly

When the cold hits, they're out
to vacation down south,
then back north, for the warmth of the sun

First fly the males
to prepare the details
to impress the females when they come

When Miss Ellie arrived
and met a male called Clive
    he was diving about to impress

Bits and pieces she mixed
    lots of leaves, grass, and sticks
        to build her new babies a nest

Two eggs Ellie laid
and on them she stayed
keeping them warm and protected

The only time she would leave
was to forage and feed
and then back on the nest, as expected

The babies arrived
Unlike Ellie and Clive,
they were tiny, short-beaked, and blind

Ellie dropped food
down the throats of the brood
They'd be flying in just three weeks time

Lily learned too
that the hummingbird crew
have a job which is called pollination

Their long beaks collect the
lovely sweet nectar
while leaving a pollen donation

Lily learned many facts
read each book front to back
like their wings move so fast that they hum

Over three hundred types
many colors and stripes
and a group of them are known as a "charm"

They weigh very little
even less than a nickel
and they eat up to twice their own weight

They are symbols of luck,
they can't walk, hop, or cluck,
but they can fly backwards, how great

(*No other birds can fly backwards, just them)

The summer's end is now here
so begins the school year
and Lily has plenty to share

"The binoculars I found,
took me all the way down
a path about birds of the air"

Hummingbirds are amazing
their wing speed is blazing
their colors and beauty do beckon

You can never see one
poke out their tongue
it's in and out twenty times every second

Now Lily's grown up
but the birds brought her luck
she became a successful ornithologist

That's a very big word
but it means "study birds,"
and birds are where all Lily's knowledge is

Now that you know
the whole hummingbird show
we hope that your eyes opened wide

there's magic all around
and journeys abound
Lily's started with Ellie and Clive

# About the Author

Deborah Ades earned a certificate in Natural Science Illustration from the New York Botanical Gardens. Deborah has been drawing and painting as long for as she can remember. While living in Manhattan, she recalls running to catch a subway when she noticed a large dragonfly lying on the sidewalk. This began a lifelong fascination with the natural world. As a long-time lover of children's literature, Deborah wanted to contribute to the genre with her art. For her first book, Hummingbird Lily, she chose the Ruby-throated Hummingbird because it is the only hummingbird that breeds in eastern North America, making it possible for her to observe it during the warm months. Next stop, more nature, fantasy, and adventure.

## Acknowledgments

Inspired by Stephanie Ades
Book design, story adaptation, writing, and editing by Simon Mills

Scan the QR code with your phone camera to find more titles like this from
Imagine and Wonder

MIX
Paper from
responsible sources
FSC® C017606

**Replacement assurance**
If your copy fails to meet our high standards, please inform us and we will gladly replace it. admin@imagineandwonder.com

**Your guarantee of quality**
As publishers, we strive to produce every book to the highest commercial standards. The printing and binding have been planned to ensure a sturdy, attractive publication which should give years of enjoyment.

Printed in China by Hung Hing Off-set Printing Co. Ltd.

Scan the QR code to find other
amazing adventures and more from
www.ImagineAndWonder.com

IMAGINE & WONDER